Studio Fun International
An imprint of Printers Row Publishing Group
A division of Readerlink Distribution Services, LLC
10350 Barnes Canyon Road, Suite 100, San Diego, CA 92121
www.studiofun.com

Printers Row Publishing Group is a division of Readerlink Distribution Services, LLC.
Studio Fun International is a registered trademark of Readerlink Distribution Services, LLC.

All notations of errors or omissions should be addressed to Studio Fun International, Editorial Department, at the above address.

ISBN: 978-0-7944-4569-0
Manufactured, printed, and assembled in Dongguan, China.
First printing, July 2019. RRD/07/19
23 22 21 20 19   1 2 3 4 5

Disney
ALICE
in
WONDERLAND

studio fun

INTERNATIONAL

One summer day, a young girl named Alice found herself trapped with a history lesson. While her sister read of ancient kings, Alice crowned her cat Dinah. The day was simply too splendid for lessons, thought Alice.

As soon as she could, Alice slipped away from her lesson.

"Oh, Dinah," she sighed, "in my world there would be no lessons. All would be nonsense."

As Alice dreamed of her wonderland, a well-dressed white rabbit ran past.

"I'm late! I'm late!" the White Rabbit cried. Alice raced after him. "He must be going to something awfully important, like a party," she told Dinah. They followed the White Rabbit to a rabbit hole.

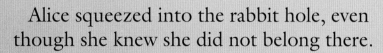

Alice squeezed into the rabbit hole, even though she knew she did not belong there.

"After all," she said, "curiousity often leads to...TROUBBBBLLLE!"

Alice's voice disappeared into a dark hole along with the rest of her. Alice floated down through the darkness. As a lamp drifted past, Alice turned it on and looked about her.

As Alice landed, a pair of white rabbit feet raced past her.

"Oh, wait, Mister Rabbit, please!" Alice called. She raced down a hallway as the White Rabbit slammed a door behind him. Alice followed him through smaller and smaller doors. "Curiouser and curiouser," Alice said.

At the last and smallest door, Alice twisted the knob. A nose wiggled under her hand! What a strange place, Alice thought. She asked the Doorknob if she could go through. "Sorry," said the Doorknob. "You're much too big."

"Why don't you try the bottle on the table?" the Doorknob suggested.

A glass bottle labeled "Drink Me" appeared. With each sip, Alice shrank. Now she could fit through the door. But the door was locked!

Tiny Alice couldn't unlock the door. She then ate a magic cookie that made her into giant Alice, but giant Alice couldn't fit through the door. She began to cry, and her tremendous tears flooded the room. Alice shrank herself again, and floated through the door's keyhole.

A wave swept Alice into a very odd race. Fish
and birds ran around a dodo, trying to get dry
while the waves kept them wet. Alice spotted
the White Rabbit again.

"Mister Rabbit!" she called.

Alice chased the White Rabbit until she was deep in a wood. Instead of finding the White Rabbit, she found a pair of twins.

"I'm Tweedledee," said one. "I'm Tweedledum," said the other.

"I'm following the White Rabbit." Alice told Tweedledee and Tweedledum. "I'm curious to know where he's going."

Tweedledum sighed. "It can be dangerous, to be too curious."

"I am sure you are right," said Alice, but nevertheless hurried off to find the White Rabbit.

To Alice's surprise, the White Rabbit found her. "I'm late!" he said. "Go get my gloves!"

Inside his cottage, Alice found cookies labeled "Eat Me." Happily, Alice helped herself. Soon, she felt herself growing…and growing…

…and growing, until her arms and legs stuck out of the White Rabbit's cottage!

"HELP! Monster!" The White Rabbit ran for the Dodo.

The Dodo suggested burning down the house!

Alice ate a carrot from the Rabbit's garden
and shrank to a tiny size again. As the Dodo
asked her for a match, the White Rabbit ran off
once more.

"Oh, dear," puffed tiny Alice, "I'll never catch
him!"

Alice ran out of the garden and came upon
a caterpillar making smoky vowels.
"Who are you?" he asked, puffing out a U.
Alice blew his smoke away—and blew the
caterpillar right out of his clothes!

Alice was worried until she saw that the caterpillar had become a butterfly.

As the new butterfly flew away, he told her, "One side of the mushroom will make you grow taller, and the other side will make you grow shorter."

Alice broke off two pieces of the mushroom. "I wonder which side is which," she said. With a shrug, Alice bit into the first mushroom piece.

Normal-sized again, Alice tucked the leftover mushroom pieces in her pocket. She searched for some sign of the White Rabbit. She did find signs, but they didn't help. As Alice puzzled which way to go, she heard singing.

Alice looked up and saw a large mouth grinning down at her. Bit by bit, the body of a Cheshire Cat appeared.

"If you'd really like to know," he said, "the White Rabbit went that way. Of course, if I were looking for a White Rabbit, I'd ask the Mad Hatter. Or there's the March Hare. Of course, he's mad, too. Most everyone's mad here."

Alice walked on until she heard more singing. That must be the Mad Hatter and the March Hare, she thought.

As the tea-for-twosome wished each other "Merry Unbirthday!" Alice tried to join them. But the pair shouted, "No room!"

"Oh, I'm very sorry," said Alice. "But I did enjoy your singing."

"You enjoyed our singing?" asked the March Hare.

"What a delightful child!" exclaimed the Mad Hatter.

The Mad Hatter swept off his hat and wished Alice a "Merry Unbirthday." There, on top of his head, was an unbirthday cake!

"Now blow out the candle and make your wish," said the Mad Hatter.

As if in answer to Alice's wish, the White Rabbit appeared. "I'm late!" he cried.

The Mad Hatter and the March Hare decided that the Rabbit's watch must be broken. So they fixed it with jam and lemon!

Alice shook her head and walked away.
"I've had enough nonsense," she said. But
she couldn't find her path home. Above her,
Alice heard the Cheshire Cat again.

"I want to go home," Alice told him.

The Cheshire Cat opened a door in the
tree. Alice stepped through, into the world
of the Queen of Hearts.

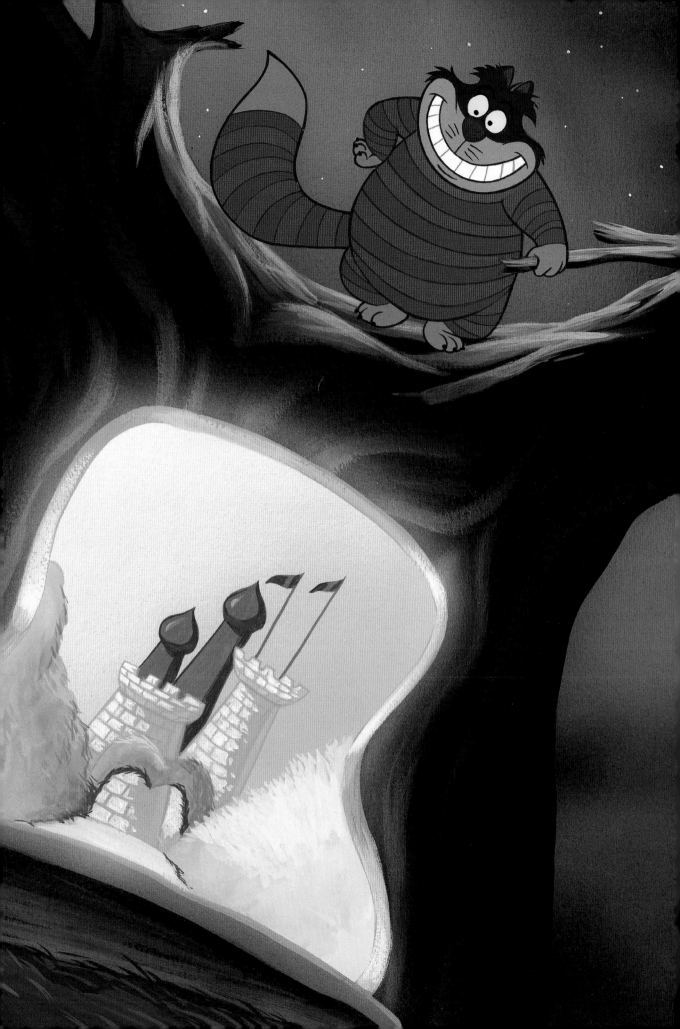

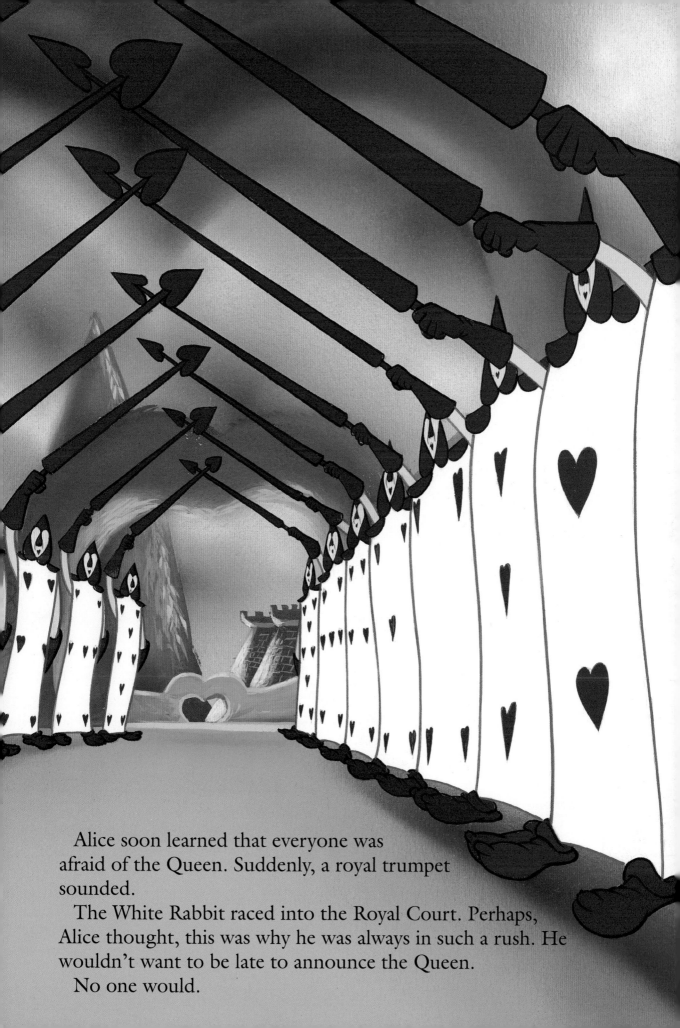

Alice soon learned that everyone was
afraid of the Queen. Suddenly, a royal trumpet
sounded.

The White Rabbit raced into the Royal Court. Perhaps,
Alice thought, this was why he was always in such a rush. He
wouldn't want to be late to announce the Queen.

No one would.

"Her Imperial Highness!" called the White Rabbit. "The Queen of Hearts!"

The cards cheered as the Queen entered. Trailing behind her, the King cleared his throat.

"And the King," the White Rabbit added.

The Queen spotted Alice. "Why, it's a little girl! Now where are you from and where are you going?"

"I'm trying to find my way home," Alice answered.

"Your way!" the Queen shouted. "All ways here are my ways!"

The Queen calmed down when she learned that Alice
played croquet. The Queen loved croquet. The cards always
made sure she won.

As the Queen prepared to swing, the Cheshire Cat
appeared, but only Alice could see him.

"You know," he told Alice, "we could make her really angry."
"Oh, no!" said Alice. "Stop!"
The Cheshire Cat tangled the Queen's skirt and tripped her up. As she flopped down, her skirt flapped up.

The Queen heaved herself up. "Someone's head will roll for this! Yours!" she bellowed at Alice.

The King pulled on the Queen's skirt. "Couldn't she have a little trial first?"

The Queen harumphed, but said yes.

The White Rabbit read the charge: Alice had caused the Queen of Hearts to lose her temper.

"Are you ready for your sentence?" the Queen asked Alice.

"Sentence?" said Alice. "Oh, but there must be a verdict first."

"Sentence first!" the Queen thundered.
"Off with her head!"

Alice found the mushroom pieces in her
pocket and stuck them in her mouth. She
grew until she towered over the Queen.

"I'm not afraid of you!" Alice said to the
Queen.

Suddenly, Alice felt herself shrinking!
"Off with her head!" the Queen shouted once more.
The court of cards closed in on Alice. She raced away,
into a maze. She escaped the maze, and found herself
back in the Dodo's beach race!

The cards chased Alice down the beach. In the wisps of smoke, Alice saw the Doorknob and his little door.

She tugged on the Doorknob. "I simply must get out!" she gasped.

"But you are outside," the Doorknob said.

Alice peered through the keyhole. There she was, sleeping in the meadow where she had heard her history lesson!

"Alice!" Alice's sister woke her. "It's time for tea."

Alice looked around. Her wonderland—with its angry Queen—was gone.

Alice shook away her dream and smiled. The day was simply too splendid for nonsense!